BIG BROTHER BLUES

by Jon Chardiet • Illustrated by Charles Micucci

❄ ❄ ❄

To Cole with love, from Poppy — J.C.

To Pat and Mike — C.M.

No part of this publication may be reproduced, or stored in a retrieval system, or transmitted in any form or by any means, electronic, mechanical, photocopying, recording, or otherwise, without written permission of the publisher. For information regarding permissions, write to Scholastic Inc., Attention: Permissions Department, 555 Broadway, New York, NY 10012.

Text copyright ©1998 by Chardiet Unlimited, Inc. Illustrations copyright ©1998 by Charles Micucci. All rights reserved. Published by Scholastic Inc. SCHOLASTIC, CARTWHEEL BOOKS and the CARTWHEEL BOOKS logo are trademarks and/or registered trademarks of Scholastic Inc.

Library of Congress Cataloging-in-Publication Data

Chardiet, Jon.
    Parker Penguin, big brother blues / by Jon Chardiet ; illustrated by Charles Micucci.
       p.   cm.—(Read with me)
       "Cartwheel Books."
    Summary: Parker Penguin complains that his baby brother has an easy life with no responsibilities, so his parents put things in perspective for him by treating Parker like a baby for an afternoon.
    ISBN 0-590-14924-5
    [1. Babies—Fiction. 2. Brother—Fiction. 3. Penguins—Fiction.] I. Micucci, Charles, ill. II. Title. III. Series: Read with me (New York, N.Y.).
PZ7.C37365Pat 1998
[E]—dc21

98-34154
CIP
AC

10 9 8 7 6 5 4 3 2 1   8 9/9 0/0 01 02 03

Printed in the U.S.A.
First printing, November 1998

On the first day of first grade, Mr. Owly was giving a homework assignment when Parker complained.
"Why do we have to do homework?" he asked loudly.

Mr. Owly thought a while before he spoke.
"Young Master Penguin!" he said. "Homework is your responsibility as a first grader! You'll never grow up until you accept your responsibility!"
"If growing up means having to do homework every day— I don't want to!" said Parker.

As they walked home, Parker and Billy Bear complained about all the work they had to do.

"I wish I were little again!" said Parker. "My little brother doesn't have to pick up his toys, fold his pants, or make his bed!"

"*I* have to put all my toys away after I play with them!

I have to put my dirty clothes in the hamper! *And* I have to make my bed *every* day or I don't get any allowance! And now I have to do homework, too!"

"At dinner, my little brother doesn't get punished when he plays with his food — and he never has to finish anything!"

"But if I play with my food, I get punished. I always have to clear my plate or I don't get dessert. And I have to help with the dishes even if my favorite television show is on!"

"That's what you get for being born first!" said Billy. "I'll come over to your house after dinner and we can play hockey."

When Parker got home, he ran into the kitchen to get some milk and cookies.

"Wait a minute, young man!" said Mama Penguin. "You didn't make your bed this morning! Before you can have a snack, you must take care of your responsibilities."

So Parker picked up his room and made his bed. Then, he took out the trash. And then he shoveled snow in the front yard.

When he was finished, his mother said, "Now get started on your homework, and I'll bring you a nice cold glass of milk and a plate of cookies."

"It's just not fair!" cried Parker. "I always have to do everything and Junior doesn't ever do anything. Why does he get all the special treatment?"

Mama Penguin thought for a minute. "Would you like to be treated the same as Junior?"

"Yes!" cried Parker.

"Okay," said Mama Penguin. "Come with me."

Mama Penguin dressed Parker like a two-year-old. First, she took off his helmet.

"Hey!" cried Parker. "That's my lucky hockey helmet!"

"Babies don't wear helmets," said Mama Penguin, "but they do wear bonnets."

Then Mama Penguin carried him upstairs and put him in the crib.

"Now you are going to nap for an hour so you won't be cranky."

"But my favorite cartoon comes on in twenty minutes!" cried Parker.

"Babies don't have favorite cartoons," said Mama Penguin. "And besides, I can't understand what you're saying anyway, since babies only speak baby talk."

"Gaboo gaba!" yelled Parker's little brother.

Parker stayed in the crib for what seemed like days. He was so bored that he wished he could shovel snow, or clean his room, or even do his homework. But all he did was lie in the crib, staring at the ceiling.

Finally, he fell asleep.

Soon Parker's father came home.
Parker woke up and ran downstairs.
"Hey, Dad!" he cried.
Papa Penguin picked him up in his arms.
"Look at my eensy, weensy baby Penguin!"
he said. He tickled Parker under the chin.
"Itchee gitchee goo!" said Papa Penguin.
"Hey, Dad!" yelled Parker. "Cut it out!"

"Does my little boy want to play?" said Papa Penguin.
"Yeah!" said Parker. "Let's play hockey!"
But Papa Penguin just took Parker outside and stuck him in the baby swing.

"Hey, Dad!" screamed Parker. "Knock it off! The whole neighborhood is going to see me dressed like this! I'll never be able to show my face in public again!"

Papa Penguin pushed him higher and higher. Soon all the neighbors were watching.

Just then, Mama Penguin called from the kitchen, "It's dinnertime!"

"Meatloaf and mashed potatoes with carrots and peas! My favorite!" said Papa Penguin as he carried Parker inside under one arm.

"Mine, too!" yelled Parker.

Papa Penguin put Parker in the high chair and tied a bib around his neck. Mama Penguin served the food. She gave Parker a baby bottle.

"I don't want this!" yelled Parker. "I want meatloaf!"

But Mama Penguin ignored him.

Parker took a sip of the baby bottle.

"This stuff is gross!" Parker threw the bottle on the ground.

Mama Penguin opened a jar of baby food and emptied it into a bowl.

"Open wide," she said. "Here comes the train into the tunnel!"

Parker took a bite. "Ugh!" said Parker. "This tastes terrible!"

He was so angry, he hit the bowl. It flipped through the air...

. . . and landed on his head. Everybody laughed — except for Parker.

"Bad baby," said Papa Penguin. "It's time to put you in your playpen."

"Chocolate cake for dessert," said Mama Penguin.

"Yaay!" said Papa Penguin.

Parker sat in the playpen, watching his parents eat Mama Penguin's famous chocolate cake.
Just then, the doorbell rang.
"Who is it?" asked Mama Penguin.

It was Billy Bear and all his friends!

"Hi, Mrs. Penguin," said Billy. "Can Parker come out and play hockey?"

"Ask him yourself!" said Mama Penguin.

When they saw Parker, everybody laughed. They laughed so hard that even Parker had to laugh.

"Wait!" said Parker.

"I guess I was jealous of my baby brother because he didn't have any responsibilities," said Parker. "But now I see that I get to do a lot of things he can't. I get to ride my bike, and play hockey, and eat real food, and even do my homework! Mr. Owly was right. I wouldn't want to be a baby again for anything!"

"Hooray!" said Mama Penguin. "My big boy is back!"

"Can I have some chocolate cake now?" asked Parker.

"Baa baa," said Junior.

Everybody laughed.

Everyone had chocolate cake. Even Junior got a piece. But since he was just a baby, he put it on his head.